DK

T0011258

SPIDER-MAN

POCKET EXPERT

Written by Catherine Saunders

CONTENTS

INTRODUCTION

Come and meet Spider-Man. Actually, it's Spider-Men, and don't forget the Spider-Women (and Spider-pigs)! It's a tiny bit complicated, but don't worry—this book has EVERYTHING you need to know. Find out all about Peter Parker, Miles Morales, and a host of other spider-y Super Heroes, plus get to know their friends, foes, and a few folks who just can't make up their minds one way or the other.

Use the A–Z contents list above to find your favorite Super Hero or Villain, and check out the glossary on p.78 for any unfamiliar words.

PETER PARKER

⚡ RATING

FIGHTING SKILLS
●●●●●●●○

SPEED
●●●●●●●○

STRENGTH
●●●●●●●○

Peter Parker was a high school student who loved science and hated sports. A bite from a radioactive spider changed his life overnight. It gave him amazing powers. And with that came great responsibilities...

KEY ABILITIES

- ☑ Science
- ☑ Inventing
- ☑ Teaching
- ☑ Photography
- ☑ Keeping secrets

WHEN HE'S SPIDEY, PETER NEEDS A MASK SO THAT NO ONE KNOWS HIS TRUE IDENTITY

PETER WEARS HIS SPIDEY COSTUME UNDER HIS REGULAR CLOTHES

SPIDEY SECRET

Peter used his science knowledge to engineer web-shooters for his wrists. He also designed a costume and called himself "Spider-Man."

SECRET IDENTITY

Peter knew that it would put his family at risk if he told them about his powers. So he kept them secret from everyone.

SPIDER-MAN

At first, Peter used his powers to find fame as a wrestler, but he soon realized that was not who he wanted to be. Now, whenever his spider-sense tells him that someone is in trouble, he'll do whatever he can to help.

⚡ RATING

FIGHTING SKILLS
●●●●●●○○

SPEED
●●●●●●○○

STRENGTH
●●●●●●○○

WEB-SLINGER

Spidey uses his web-shooters to swing above the city. His feet and hands can also stick to most surfaces, which makes wall-crawling easy, too.

THE SPIDER BITE TRANSFORMED PETER'S BODY, MAKING HIM STRONG AND AGILE

WRIST SHOOTERS CONTAIN WEBS THAT CAN STICK TO ANYTHING OR EVEN WRAP UP VILLAINS

KEY ABILITIES

Name: Peter Parker

☑ Agility

☑ Reflexes

☑ Healing power

☑ Spider-sense warns of danger

SPIDEY SECRET

Peter Parker goes to university and then gets a job as a photographer on the *Daily Bugle* newspaper. He always seems to get great shots of Spider-Man...

5

MILES MORALES

⚡ RATING

FIGHTING SKILLS
●●●●●●○

SPEED
●●●●●●●○

STRENGTH
●●●●●●○

Teenager Miles Morales was just trying to adjust to a new school and make friends when a spider bite changed his life. Sound familiar? Miles has a lot to learn, but at least he has Peter Parker (and several other spider-heroes) who understand exactly how he feels.

MILES IS NOT SURE HE CAN BE SPIDER-MAN...

OUCH!

The spider that bites Miles had hitched a ride with Miles' uncle Aaron, aka the Prowler.

SPIDEY SECRET

At first, Miles doesn't want to be a Super Hero. It's dangerous and stressful, and he knows his dad wouldn't like it.

...BUT IF HE'S GOING TO BE SPIDEY, HE WANTS HIS OWN LOOK

🧠 KEY ABILITIES

☑ Science
☑ Math
☑ Graffiti art
☑ Sense of humor
☑ Facing up to problem

SPIDER-MAN

Miles Morales has all of Peter's amazing powers, plus two useful extras of his own—spider-camouflage and "venom blasts." With his spider-camouflage, Miles can be almost invisible and he can also temporarily paralyze foes with his venom blasts.

⚡ RATING

FIGHTING SKILLS
●●●●●●○○

SPEED
●●●●●●○○

STRENGTH
●●●●●●○○

MILES WEARS HIS WEB-SHOOTERS ON HIS WRISTS

MILES HAS MASTERED WEB SWINGING AND WALL-CRAWLING

KEY ABILITIES

Name: Miles Morales
- ☑ Spider-camouflage
- ☑ Venom blasts
- ☑ Agility
- ☑ Healing power
- ☑ Spider-sense

SPIDEY SECRET

Miles improved his combat skills by watching videos of Peter Parker's past battles and studying his moves.

BEING HIMSELF

There are many different spider-heroes in many different universes, but Miles is working out exactly what kind of Spider-Man he wants to be.

AARON DAVIS

Aaron Davis might be a criminal with some very bad friends, but he is also Miles Morales' uncle. He loves his nephew and offers him advice and encouragement when he needs it.

⚡ RATING

FIGHTING SKILLS
●●●●●●●○

SPEED
●●●●●●○○

STRENGTH
●●●●●●●○

FAMILY ISSUES

When the Prowler and Spider-Man clash, neither one knows whom they're really fighting.

MILES WOULD NEVER GUESS THAT HIS COOL AND CALM UNCLE IS THE PROWLER

🧠 KEY ABILITIES

Alias: the Prowler

☑ Master thief
☑ Athlete
☑ Expert acrobat
☑ Expert martial artist

CASUAL CLOTHES

SPIDEY SECRET

When Aaron is committing crimes he becomes the Prowler to hide his true identity.

AUNT MAY PARKER

When Peter Parker's parents go missing, presumed dead, his aunt and uncle welcome him into their home. After Uncle Ben is killed by a burglar, Aunt May raises Peter alone.

⚡ RATING

FIGHTING SKILLS
●●●●●●●○○○

SPEED
●●●●●●○○○○

STRENGTH
●●●●●●○○○○

GETTING MARRIED

After Ben's death, May finds love with Jay Jameson, father of J. Jonah Jameson. Unlike his son, Jay is a big fan of Spidey.

KIND, HARDWORKING UNCLE

⚙ KEY TRAITS

Name: Maybelle Parker

☑ Practical
☑ Responsible
☑ Caring
☑ Resourceful
☑ Supportive

SPIDEY SECRET

Before marrying Jay Jameson, Aunt May unwittingly romanced several villains, including Doc Ock.

CARING AND SUPPORTIVE AUNT

BLACK CAT

⚡ RATING

FIGHTING SKILLS
●●●●●●○

SPEED
●●●●●●○

STRENGTH
●●●●●●○

GLOVES
CONTAIN
RETRACTABLE
CLAWS

Black Cat is a reformed (mostly) burglar. Like a cat, she is stealthy, agile, and cunning—skills that made her a successful burglar, but also a great asset to any Super Hero team.

FRIEND OR FOE?

Spidey has been a good influence on Black Cat, but sometimes the two friends still fight on different sides.

SPIDEY SECRET

Tinkerer designed Black Cat's costume to enhance her natural speed, strength, and agility.

COSTUME IS
MADE OF
FLEXIBLE
MATERIAL

KEY ABILITIES

Name: Felicia Hardy

☑ Athlete

☑ Martial artist

☑ Safecracking/lock picking

☑ Manipulating her surroundings to bring bad luck on others

BLACK PANTHER

T'Challa is not just the king of Wakanda, he is also his country's warrior champion, Black Panther. He wears a special Vibranium suit which absorbs impact and protects him from injury.

PANTHER-LIKE CLAWS IN GLOVES

⚡ RATING

FIGHTING SKILLS
●●●●●●●○

SPEED
●●●●●●●○

STRENGTH
●●●●●●●○

KEY ABILITIES

Name: T'Challa

☑ Genius-level intelligence
☑ Tactics and strategy
☑ Enhanced senses
☑ Tracking
☑ Healing

SPIDEY SECRET

Black Panther gains his super-powers from a special plant that grows only in Wakanda.

VIBRANIUM PADS ON HANDS AND FEET PROVIDE EXTRA GRIP

LEADER

Black Panther has worked with Spidey as part of the Avengers. Black Panther led the team for a while.

11

BLACK WIDOW

⚡ RATING

FIGHTING SKILLS
●●●●●●●○

SPEED
●●●●●●●○

STRENGTH
●●●●●●●○

Black Widow is a former Russian spy who often works with Spider-Man as part of the Avengers. She's tough, brave, and extremely agile, and also uses her spy skills to assist SHIELD when needed.

KEY ABILITIES

Name: Natalia Romanova/
Natasha Romanoff

☑ Enhanced speed and strength
☑ Weapons expert
☑ Gymnast

WRIST GAUNTLETS CONTAIN VARIOUS WEAPONS

AMAZING FLEXIBILITY

SPIDEY SECR

Black Widow gets her n
from the Black Widow
program that gave h
enhanced abilities

TEACHER

Black Widow also helps to train Miles Morales and his Champions teammates.

CAPTAIN AMERICA

Captain America understands better than most how Peter felt when he became Spider-Man. Cap's own body was transformed by Super-Soldier Serum and his life changed dramatically.

RATING

FIGHTING SKILLS
●●●●●●●

SPEED
●●●●●●●

STRENGTH
●●●●●●●

BEHIND THE SUIT

Sometimes, Cap likes to ride his motorcycle and try to remember what it feels like to be an ordinary person.

ICONIC COSTUME IS INSTANTLY RECOGNIZABLE

CAP IS ALWAYS READY FOR ACTION

KEY ABILITIES

Name: Steve Rogers

- ☑ Enhanced human physique
- ☑ Master of martial arts
- ☑ Skilled acrobat
- ☑ Master tactician

CAP'S SHIELD IS MADE FROM VIBRANIUM, A RARE AND POWERFUL METAL

SPIDEY SECRET

Peter admires Cap for his bravery and wisdom, and Cap has great respect for the younger hero, too.

HERO

CAPTAIN MARVEL

⚡ RATING

FIGHTING SKILLS
●●●●●●○○○

SPEED
●●●●●●○○○

STRENGTH
●●●●●●○○○

Former US Air Force pilot, astronaut, and intelligence agent, Carol Danvers was a pretty impressive person even before an accident turned her into a human-Kree hybrid with super-powers.

TEAM PLAYER

Captain Marvel and Spidey have been friends for years and often team up in the New Avengers.

CAROL CAN BLAST PHOTON ENERGY FROM HER FINGERTIPS

KEY ABILITIES

Name: Carol Danvers

☑ Flight, even in space

☑ Healing

☑ Durability

☑ Control, absorb, and discharge energy

SPIDEY SECRET

Before she took on the name Captain Marvel, Carol Danvers was known as Ms. Marvel.

HER SUIT DOES NOT HAVE SUPER-HUMAN DURABILITY

CARNAGE

When part of the alien symbiote Venom attached itself to vicious criminal Cletus Kasady, the result was a powerful and relentless Super Villain. Worse still, it absolutely hates Spider-Man.

⚡ RATING

FIGHTING SKILLS
●●●●●●○

SPEED
●●●●●●○

STRENGTH
●●●●●●○

KEY ABILITIES

Name: Cletus Kasady
- ☑ No regard for human life
- ☑ Enormous strength
- ☑ Create sharp weapons or long tentacles with its body

SPIDEY SECRET

Carnage is able to neutralize Spidey's spider-sense, leaving the web-slinger vulnerable to attack.

CARNAGE CAN GENERATE LONG TENDRILS TO TRAP AN OPPONENT

DISTINCTIVE RED FORM

DEADLY ENEMY

It's hard to know who Carnage hates more, Spidey or Venom. In any case, it is stronger than both of them combined.

VILLAIN

CHAMELEON

One of Spider-Man's oldest foes, Chameleon can copy anyone's appearance. His career as a spy was thwarted by Spidey, so he became a master criminal instead. Naturally, he now hates Spider-Man.

⚡ RATING

FIGHTING SKILLS
●●●●●●●○○○

SPEED
●●●●●●●○○○

STRENGTH
●●●●●●●○○○

CHAMELEON IS NO LONGER SURE WHO HE REALLY IS

SPIDEY SECRET

Chameleon is the half brother of Sergei Kravinoff, aka Kraven the Hunter, but they are not close.

MASTERMIND

Chameleon can keep up his disguises for months at a time and he has impersonated Spidey many times.

🧠 KEY ABILITIES

Name: Dmitri Smerdyakov

☑ Disguise

☑ Mimicry

☑ Spying

☑ Increased lifespan

A SPECIAL SERUM GIVES CHAMELEON THE POWER TO ALTER HIS BODY

DOCTOR DOOM

Doctor Doom combines the powers of science and sorcery. He's brilliant but bitter and determined to take over the world, starting with his home country of Latveria.

DOOM HIDES BEHIND AN IRON MASK

⚡ RATING

FIGHTING SKILLS
●●●●●●○

SPEED
●●●●●●●

STRENGTH
●●●●●●○

KEY ABILITIES

Name: Victor von Doom

☑ Genius-level intelligence
☑ Magic
☑ Martial arts
☑ Weapons expert

SPIDEY SECRET

Victor wrongly blames Reed Richards of the Fantastic Four for an accident that left him scarred.

TITANIUM ARMOR WITH NUCLEAR-POWERED WEAPONS

WORTHY FOE

As Reed Richards' friend, Spidey is naturally Doctor Doom's enemy and part of his quest for revenge. It seems that Doom may have won this round...

DOCTOR OCTOPUS

Doc Ock is an evil genius who controls four steel tentacles with his mind. He'll try anything to defeat Spider-Man, from creating an army of Octobots to romancing Peter's Aunt May!

⚡ RATING

FIGHTING SKILLS
●●●●●●○

SPEED
●●●●●●○

STRENGTH
●●●●●●○

EXTENDABLE TENTACLES

SPIDEY SECRET

Doc Ock got his super-human powers when a lab experiment went wrong.

KEY ABILITIES

Name: Dr. Otto Octavius
☑ Scientific genius
☑ Agility
☑ Strategy and plannin
☑ Super-strength

NEW PLAN

Doc Ock has even tried becoming Spider-Man, but he's just not cut out to be a Super Hero.

POWERFUL, ROTATING PINCERS

18

DOCTOR STRANGE

As Earth's Sorcerer Supreme, Doctor Strange is a master of magic. He's a great friend to Spidey and can instantly appear in spirit form whenever the web-slinger needs his advice.

RATING

FIGHTING SKILLS
●●●●●●●

SPEED
●●●●●●●

STRENGTH
●●●●●●●

IN PERSON

When Spidey needs back up, Doctor Strange can teleport right into the action to help.

ENERGY BLAST

SPIDEY SECRET

Doctor Strange was a brilliant (but arrogant) surgeon until a car accident ended that career.

KEY ABILITIES

Name: Dr. Stephen Strange

- ☑ Magic
- ☑ Martial arts
- ☑ Energy manipulation
- ☑ Teleportation
- ☑ Controlling time

CAPE OF LEVITATION

19

VILLAIN

ELECTRO

⚡ RATING

FIGHTING SKILLS
●●●●●●●○

SPEED
●●●●●●●○

STRENGTH
●●●●●●●○

An accident left Max Dillon with the power to generate and control electricity. He can black out a whole city in seconds, and he can recharge his powers from any electrical source.

SPIDEY SECRET

Electro has one major weakness—water can short circuit his powers. Spidey uses this whenever he can.

ELECTRO CAN BLAST LIGHTNING AT HIS ENEMIES

COSTUME PROTECTS ELECTRO BUT SHOCKS ANYONE WHO TOUCHES IT

🧠 KEY ABILITIES

Name: Maxwell Dillon

☑ Generating electricity

☑ Projecting lightning bolts

☑ Traveling by "riding" on electricity

🕸 SHOCKING!

Even Spidey has no defense against an electric shock, but he has still been able to defeat Electro in their many battles.

20

FLASH THOMPSON

Eugene "Flash" Thompson is a reformed school bully who is now one of Peter Parker's closest friends. He got super-powers from the symbiote Venom, but uses them for good. He is known as Agent Anti-Venom.

⚡ RATING

FIGHTING SKILLS
●●●●●●○

SPEED
●●●●●●●

STRENGTH
●●●●●●○

CHANGING

Flash used to bully Peter, but he's changed. He served in the US Army and is one of Spidey's most loyal supporters.

FLASH DEVELOPED HIS COMBAT SKILLS IN THE ARMY

SPIDEY SECRET

Before Flash knew that Peter was Spider-Man, he was part of a Spider-Man fan club!

THE NTI-VENOM PROTECTS SH AND CAN AL OTHERS TOO

Y ABILITIES

nes:
- ene "Flash" Thompson/ nt Anti-Venom
- Super-human stamina
- Durability
- Some Spidey-like powers
- Healing

FUSION

⚡ RATING

FIGHTING SKILLS
●●●●●●○○

SPEED
●●●●●●○○

STRENGTH
●●●●●●○○

Fusion can make people believe anything he wants them to. At first he used this skill to make lots and lots of money. Now he's achieved that, he uses his powers of illusion to try and destroy Spider-Man.

FUSION'S MIND IS HIS GREATEST WEAPON

KEY ABILITIES

Name: Wayne Markley

☑ Persuasion

☑ Illusion

☑ Intelligence

☑ Explosives expert

SPIDEY SECRET

Fusion's son died in an accident while trying to copy his hero Spidey. That's why Fusion hates Spider-Man.

SUIT TRANSFORMS INTO WHATEVER FUSION WANTS

FAKING IT

Fusion has the power to make Spider-Man believe he is seriously hurt. But Spidey soon realizes it's an illusion.

GANKE LEE

Ganke Lee is Miles Morales'
school roommate and best
friend. Ganke knows Miles' secret
and helps his friend figure out
how to balance being a Super
Hero and a teenager.

⚡ RATING

FIGHTING SKILLS
●●●●●●●○○○

SPEED
●●●●●●●○○○

STRENGTH
●●●●●●●○○○

WORKING IT OUT

Ganke helps Miles to
understand his
powers, and offers
advice on what the
rookie hero should do.

> What?
> Wow.
> Yes.

LIKE MILES,
GANKE HAS HIS
OWN STYLE

SPIDEY SECRET

Ganke is a huge Super Hero fan.
He likes Spidey, of course, but
his real favorite is Goldballs
from the X-Men.

EVERY TEEN
NEEDS A
BACKPACK

⚙ KEY TRAITS

Alias: Ned (it's a long story)
- ☑ Smart
- ☑ Trustworthy
- ☑ Loyal
- ☑ Enthusiastic
- ☑ Good at keeping secrets
  (mostly)

23

GHOST-SPIDER

⚡ RATING

FIGHTING SKILLS
●●●●●●●○

SPEED
●●●●●●○○

STRENGTH
●●●●●●●○

Gwen Stacy is important to Spider-Man in many universes. However, in Earth-65 it is a teenage Gwen, not Peter Parker, who gains spider-like super-powers. She becomes Ghost-Spider, aka Spider-Woman.

TEENAGE LIFE

Gwen is friends with the non-super-powered Peter Parker in her universe. He is a big fan of Spider-Woman!

WEB-SHOOTERS DESIGNED BY JANET VAN DYNE, AKA WASP

SPIDEY SECRET

At first Gwen found it hard being a teenage Super Hero. Now she sees that her mission is to help people.

GWEN CAN TRAVEL BETWEEN THE DIFFERENT UNIVERSES

KEY ABILITIES

Name: Gwen Stacy

☑ Wall-crawling

☑ Super-human strength

☑ Super-human agility

☑ Spider-sense

GREEN GOBLIN

Businessman Norman Osborn became the Green Goblin after an experimental serum gave him super-strength. As Green Goblin, his quest for chaos and destruction has led to many battles with Spider-Man.

⚡ RATING

FIGHTING SKILLS
●●●●●●○○

SPEED
●●●●●●●○

STRENGTH
●●●●●●●○

GREEN
GOBLIN
WEARS AN
ARMORED
SUIT

KEY ABILITIES

Name: Norman Osborn

☑ Super-human agility
☑ Super-human stamina
☑ Healing/regeneration
☑ Intelligence

THE GOBLIN
GLIDER IS
JET-POWERED
AND CAN
HOVER IN
ONE SPOT

SPIDEY SECRET

Osborn was always ruthless, but the Green Goblin has taken over his personality, driving him mad.

FIRE POWER

Green Goblin fights Spidey with an explosive array of pumpkin bombs and gas grenades.

HARRY OSBORN

Harry is the son of Norman Osborn, aka the Green Goblin. Although he has been friends with Peter Parker since university, he cannot always be relied on to do the right thing. He's even taken over as Green Goblin several times.

⚡ RATING

FIGHTING SKILLS
●●●●●●●○

SPEED
●●●●●●●○

STRENGTH
●●●●●●●○

HARRY HAS CHANGED HIS APPEARANCE MANY TIMES, FROM SUPER VILLAIN TO REGULAR PERSON

JUST LIKE DAD

Taking Goblin Serum gives Harry amazing powers, but it costs him his sanity. As the Green Goblin, Harry will do anything to defeat Spidey.

KEY ABILITIES

Names: Harold Osborn

☑ Genius-level intelligence

☑ Super-human strengt[h]

☑ Super-human stamin[a] (all from Goblin Seru[m])

HERE, HARRY IS DRESSED FOR BUSINESS

SPIDEY SECRET

Harry is Peter Parker's friend, but he absolutely hates Spider-Man and is always plotting his downfall.

HOBGOBLIN

Fashion designer Roderick Kingsley will do anything to achieve success. When he found Norman Osborn's Green Goblin Serum, he didn't hesitate in taking it. It turned him into the villainous Hobgoblin.

⚡ RATING

FIGHTING SKILLS
●●●●●●○

SPEED
●●●●●●○○

STRENGTH
●●●●●●●○

CLOAK CONCEALS HOBGOBLIN'S TERRIFYING FACE

🧠 KEY ABILITIES

Name: Roderick Kingsley

- ☑ Durability
- ☑ Agility
- ☑ Healing
- ☑ Quick reflexes

SPIDEY SECRET

Spider-Man once saved Roderick when he was being attacked. But Hobgoblin still hates him!

THE SCALES ON THE ARMOR PROVIDE (STYLISH) PROTECTION

📷 GOBLIN GLIDER

Hobgoblin has the same equipment as the Green Goblin. The goblin glider gives him an advantage in this battle with Miles Morales.

HULK

⚡ RATING

FIGHTING SKILLS
●●●●●●●○

SPEED
●●●●●●●○

STRENGTH
●●●●●●●○

An accident involving gamma radiation gave scientist Bruce Banner incredible powers. Now whenever he's angry he transforms into a massive green Super Hero, Hulk.

SPIDEY SECRET

The angrier Hulk gets, the stronger he becomes. His transformation can also be triggered by stress or anxiety.

HULK'S SKIN IS BULLETPROOF

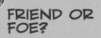

HULK CAN TRAVEL SEVERAL MILES WITH ONE LEAP

KEY ABILITIES

Name: Bruce Banner

☑ Almost limitless strength
☑ Virtually indestructible
☑ Stamina and durability
☑ Genius-level Intelligence

FRIEND OR FOE?

Hulk is an Avenger, but sometimes his unstable personality causes him to battle his friends (like Spidey) instead.

28

HUMAN TORCH

Johnny Storm got his powers during a failed space mission. Cosmic rays left him with the ability to ignite plasma across his body and become a flaming torch. He is part of the Super Hero team the Fantastic Four.

RATING

FIGHTING SKILLS
●●●●●●○

SPEED
●●●●●●○

STRENGTH
●●●●●●○

FIERY FRIENDS

Spider-Man and Johnny are good friends. It's nice to have a buddy who understands what it's like to be a Super Hero.

JOHNNY CAN CONTROL THE HEAT ENERGY WITHOUT FEELING ANY PAIN

KEY ABILITIES

Name: Johnny Storm

- ☑ Burst into flames at will
- ☑ Flight
- ☑ Fire an intense nova burst
- ☑ Shape and sculpt his flames
- ☑ Control the size and intensity of his flames

HE CAN FIRE FLAMING BURSTS OR USE THEM TO FLY

SPIDEY SECRET

Spider-Man took Johnny's place in the Fantastic Four for a while, when it seemed like the Human Torch was dead.

HYDRO-MAN

⚡ RATING

FIGHTING SKILLS
●●●●●●●○○○

SPEED
●●●●●●●○○○

STRENGTH
●●●●●●●○○○

Ship's crewman Morris Bench gained super-powers when he fell overboard and came into contact with an experimental power generator. He can now transform into a liquid Super Villain known as Hydro-Man.

DOUBLE TROUBLE

When Hydro-Man teams up with Sandman, they create an even worse problem for Spidey—Mud-Thing. Yuck!

HYDRO-MAN CAN TAKE HUMAN FORM WHEN HE WANTS TO

KEY ABILITIES

Name: Morris Bench

☑ Transform into a liquid

☑ Create water blasts

☑ Control water

☑ Travel through other liquids

HYDRO-MAN'S LIQUID FORM IS HARD TO STOP OR DAMAGE

SPIDEY SECRET

It was actually Spider-Man who caused Bench to fall overboard. Spidey was battling the villain Sub-Mariner at the time, so couldn't really help it.

INVISIBLE WOMAN

Invisible Woman can make her body disappear whenever she wants and create powerful force fields to protect others. Her calm personality and awesome powers make her a key member of the Fantastic Four.

⚡ RATING

FIGHTING SKILLS
●●●●●●○

SPEED
●●●●●●○

STRENGTH
●●●●●●○

KEY ABILITIES

Name: Sue Storm Richards
- ☑ Invisibility
- ☑ Projecting force fields
- ☑ Creating shock waves
- ☑ Detecting cosmic rays

SPECIAL MOLECULES ALLOW SUE'S SUIT TO BECOME INVISIBLE, TOO

SPIDEY SECRET

Sue is a big fan of Spider-Man and recommended him to her husband Reed Richards for the Future Foundation team.

SUE CAN MANIPULATE LIGHT TO CHANGE THE COLOR OF OBJECTS SUCH AS HER HAIR

NEW TEAM

The Fantastic Four became the Future Foundation when Spidey replaced Sue's brother the Human Torch for a while.

HERO

IRON MAN

⚡ RATING

FIGHTING SKILLS
●●●●●●○

SPEED
●●●●●●○

STRENGTH
●●●●●●○

Billionaire businessman Tony Stark is an engineering genius. He invented the first Iron Man suit to save his life. He's worn the armor many times since then and is now a full-fledged Super Hero.

🧠 KEY ABILITIES

Name: Tony Stark

☑ Genius-level intelligence

☑ Super-strength (in armor)

☑ Durability (in armor)

☑ Magnetism (in armor)

THIS MINIATURE REACTOR IS THE SUIT'S POWER SOURCE

JET-POWERED BOOTS ALLOW IRON MAN TO FLY

SPIDEY SECRET

Tony Stark invented an armored Spider-Man costume. The Iron Spider armor was last used by clones called the Scarlet Spiders.

🕸 MENTOR

Iron Man is a mentor to both Peter Parker and Miles Morales. They both work with him as part of the Avengers.

J. JONAH JAMESON

One of Spider-Man's most dedicated foes is not even a Super Villain. Newspaper editor J. Jonah Jameson thinks that Spidey is a public menace and is determined to ruin his reputation.

⚡ RATING

FIGHTING SKILLS
●●●●●●○

SPEED
●●●●●●○

STRENGTH
●●●●●●○

BITTER FOE

Jameson distrusts all costumed Super Heroes. He doesn't believe heroes like Spidey are truly good.

BAD-TEMPERED EXPRESSION

SPIDEY SECRET

Peter Parker worked for Jameson at the *Daily Bugle* newspaper, but Jameson had no idea how close he was to unmasking Spidey.

SLEEVES ROLLED UP, READY TO TAKE DOWN SPIDEY

KEY TRAITS

Name: John Jonah Jameson

- ☑ Hard working
- ☑ Tenacious
- ☑ Determined
- ☑ Stubborn

JACKAL

⚡ RATING

FIGHTING SKILLS
●●●●●●●○

SPEED
●●●●●●●○

STRENGTH
●●●●●●●○

Miles Warren is a college science professor and cloning expert. However, his secret cloning experiments usually have disastrous results. One turned him into the villainous and unstable Jackal.

JACKAL'S POINTED EARS RESEMBLE HIS NAMESAKE ANIMAL

KEY ABILITIES

Name: Miles Warren

- ☑ Genius-level intelligence
- ☑ Agility
- ☑ Super-human leaping
- ☑ Martial arts

RAZOR-SHARP CLAWS ARE TIPPED WITH POISON

SPIDEY SECRET

Jackal hates Spider-Man, but Miles Warren was Peter Parker's college science professor.

SPIDER ARMY

The Jackal developed a whole army of spider clones, but their arachnid powers did not work on Spidey.

34

JACKPOT

Sara Ehret was the first Super Hero Jackpot, but she didn't like having super-powers. She sold her costume to would-be hero Alana Jobson, who used a dangerous serum to give herself super-powers.

RATING

FIGHTING SKILLS
●●●●●●●○

SPEED
●●●●●●●○

STRENGTH
●●●●●●●○

HELPING OUT

Jackpot has worked with Spidey. She doesn't always make the right decisions, but she's still learning.

JACKPOT'S RED HAIR IS A WIG

SPIDEY SECRET

When he found out that Alana Jobson was not the real Jackpot, Spidey convinced Sara to return. He told her that Super Heroes have a responsibility to help other people.

COSTUME HAS BEEN WORN BY MORE THAN ONE HERO

KEY ABILITIES

Name: Sara Ehret/
Alana Jobson

☑ Super-strength
☑ Virtually bulletproof
☑ Durability
☑ Super speed

JEFF MORALES

⚡ RATING

FIGHTING SKILLS
●●●●●●●○

SPEED
●●●●●●●○

STRENGTH
●●●●●●●○

Miles Morales' dad, Jeff, tries hard to be a good person and a great father. As a police officer, his job is to uphold the law. He's not a fan of Super Heroes like Spidey, who just swing in and grab all the glory.

SPIDEY SECRET

As a kid, Jeff was on the wrong side of the law. Unlike his brother Aaron, though, he's changed his ways.

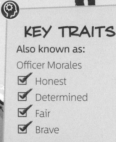

KEY TRAITS

Also known as:

Officer Morales

☑ Honest
☑ Determined
☑ Fair
☑ Brave

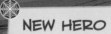
JEFF OFTEN CLASHES WITH MILES BUT ONLY BECAUSE H CARES

NEW HERO

Miles is scared to tell his dad that he's Spidey. But Jeff sees something different in the new Spider-Man.

JUGGERNAUT

Cain Marko gained super-powers from a magical ruby. Without realizing what it was, he grabbed the gem and it transformed him into Juggernaut. The villain is super tough, does not feel pain, and is virtually unstoppable.

⚡ RATING

FIGHTING SKILLS
●●●●●●○

SPEED
●●●●●●○

STRENGTH
●●●●●●○

VILLAIN FOR HIRE

Juggernaut is a tough opponent. Spider-Man has to use his brains to get the better of him.

JUGGERNAUT'S HELMET PROTECTS HIM FROM MIND CONTROL

SPIDEY SECRET

Cain hates his step brother Charles Xavier, a mutant Super Hero and leader of the X-Men.

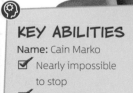

KEY ABILITIES

Name: Cain Marko

- ☑ Nearly impossible to stop
- ☑ Super-strength
- ☑ Durability and stamina
- ☑ Does not feel pain

THE MYSTICAL ARMOR IS VIRTUALLY UNBREAKABLE

37

KINGPIN

⚡ RATING

FIGHTING SKILLS
●●●●●●●○

SPEED
●●●●●●●○

STRENGTH
●●●●●●●○

Ruthless crime boss Wilson Fisk, aka Kingpin, will do anything to gain power. He doesn't care who he has to betray, swindle, or hurt—and somehow he's been elected mayor of New York City. Spider-Man has had many run-ins with this Super Villain.

KEY ABILITIES

Name: Wilson Fisk

☑ Criminal mastermind

☑ Peak human strength

☑ Multilingual

☑ Enormous willpower

SPIDEY SECRET

Spidey would love to put Kingpin in jail, but the crime boss seems to make evidence disappear.

FISK'S BULK IS PURE MUSCLE

THE CANE IS ACTUALLY A DEADLY WEAPON

FREQUENT FOE

Even two powerful Super Heroes can't get the better of Kingpin. He has Spidey and Human Torch in the palm of his hand!

KRAVEN THE HUNTER

Magical powers make Kraven a fearsome predator. However, he won't rest until he is the best hunter that has ever lived. To achieve that, he's decided that he needs to defeat the ultimate foe—Spider-Man.

⚡ RATING

FIGHTING SKILLS
●●●●●●●○

SPEED
●●●●●●●○

STRENGTH
●●●●●●●○

KRAVEN IS MORE FIERCE THAN HIS PREY!

KEY ABILITIES

Name: Sergei Kravinoff
- ☑ Tracking
- ☑ Hunting
- ☑ Super-human strength
- ☑ Super-human reflexes

SPIDEY SECRET

Kraven increases his strength by drinking magical potions, but he still can't defeat Spider-Man.

HIS BODY IS ENHANCED BY MAGIC

NEW KRAVEN

Ultimately, Sergei fails to complete his mission, so his daughter Ana takes over. She is just as determined to hunt down Spidey.

LIVING BRAIN

RATING

FIGHTING SKILLS
●●●●●●○

SPEED
●●●●●●○

STRENGTH
●●●●●●○

The Living Brain was billed as the most intelligent robot ever. It was said to know the answer to any question, including: Who is Spider-Man? However, it malfunctioned before it got a chance to reveal the secret.

ROBOT RAMPAGE

Two greedy crooks broke the Living Brain, but Spidey captured them and the renegade robot.

POWERFUL ARTIFICIAL INTELLIGENCE

SPIDEY SECRET

The Living Brain has been rebuilt several times, but it has never been able to get the better of Spidey.

CONTROL PANEL

KEY ABILITIES

Also known as: Brain

☑ Self-repairing
☑ Super-human strength
☑ Super-human durability
☑ Artificial intelligence

LIZARD

Dr. Curt Connors is a surgeon who lost his arm in a wartime bomb blast. By studying reptiles that can regenerate lost limbs, he created a secret formula that restored his arm. But it also turned him into the villain Lizard.

RATING

FIGHTING SKILLS
●●●●●●○

SPEED
●●●●●●○

STRENGTH
●●●●●●○

SPIDEY SECRET

Like Hulk's, Connors' transformation into a monster can be triggered by stress or anxiety.

RAZOR-SHARP TEETH

KEY ABILITIES

Name: Dr. Curt Connors

☑ Clinging to walls
☑ Controlling other reptiles
☑ Regenerative healing
☑ Super reflexes

TAIL CAN BE USED AS A WEAPON

IT'S COMPLICATED

Dr. Connors is friends with Spidey, but when he transforms into Lizard he has no memory of their friendship.

41

MARY AND RICHARD PARKER

Peter Parker's parents Richard and Mary were CIA agents—government-trained spies. Sadly, they died in a plane crash when he was very young, but Peter has inherited a lot of their great qualities and abilities.

⚡ RATING

FIGHTING SKILLS
●●●●●●○

SPEED
●●●●●●○

STRENGTH
●●●●●●○

SPIDEY SECRET

Apparently, Spidey's dad liked to make witty (or so he thought) puns at serious moments, too!

THEY ARE TRAINED TO DEAL WITH DANGEROUS OPPONENTS

THE PARKERS ARE A GREAT TEAM

KEY TRAITS

- ☑ Smart
- ☑ Brave
- ☑ Resourceful
- ☑ Responsible
- ☑ Good at undercover work

LOVING PARENTS

The Parkers' CIA work was very dangerous, so they always made sure that Peter was safe with his aunt and uncle.

MARY JANE WATSON

Next-door-neighbor Mary Jane Watson is the love of Peter's life. Popular, funny, and confident, MJ is the opposite of shy and awkward Peter, but their different personalities complement each other and they are a great team.

⚡ RATING

FIGHTING SKILLS
●●●●●●○○

SPEED
●●●●●●○○

STRENGTH
●●●●●●○○

RELATIONSHIP

Being close to a Super Hero is not easy. Being Spidey takes up a lot of Peter's time and energy and often puts MJ in danger.

MJ HAS DISTINCTIVE BRIGHT-RED HAIR

SPIDEY SECRET

MJ worked out Peter's secret pretty early on when she saw him leaving via his bedroom window dressed as Spidey!

KEY ABILITIES

Also known as: MJ

- ☑ Acting
- ☑ Dancing
- ☑ Running a business
- ☑ Good at keeping secrets

SHE ONCE WORKED AS TONY STARK'S ASSISTANT

43

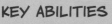
STARK

MISTER FANTASTIC

Reed Richards is a science genius who developed super-powers during a space mission. Now known as Mister Fantastic, his body can stretch and bend into any shape. Reed is a good friend and mentor to Peter Parker.

⚡ RATING

FIGHTING SKILLS
●●●●●●○

SPEED
●●●●●●○

STRENGTH
●●●●●●○

REED GOT HIS STRETCHY POWERS WHEN HE WAS EXPOSED TO COSMIC RAYS

AGREE TO DISAGREE

Even Super Heroes don't always agree. During the Super Hero Civil War, Spidey and Reed were on different sides.

SPIDEY SECRET

Reed encourages Peter Parker in his science studies and supports Spidey as he learns how to be a Super Hero.

KEY ABILITIES

Name: Dr. Reed Richards

☑ Genius-level intelligence

☑ Super-stretchy body

☑ Practically bulletproof

☑ Tying up villains with his own body

MISTER FANTASTIC'S BODY BECOMES SOFT AND STRETCHY AT WILL

MOLTEN MAN

NEUTRAL

Molten Man was created when lab assistant Mark Raxton spilt a hot liquid metallic alloy on himself. It absorbed into his skin, turning it golden and giving him super-human abilities.

⚡ RATING

FIGHTING SKILLS
●●●●●●○

SPEED
●●●●●●○

STRENGTH
●●●●●●○

SPIDEY SECRET

Molten Man's first use for his new super-powers was crime, but Spider-Man soon stopped him.

FAR TOO HOT TO HANDLE!

KEY ABILITIES

Name: Mark Raxton

- ☑ Super-human strength
- ☑ Needs little sleep
- ☑ Resistant to injury
- ☑ Creating fire
- ☑ His touch can melt or burn anything

AT FIRST THE TRANSFORMATION INTO MOLTEN MAN WAS VERY PAINFUL

🕸 HOT STUFF

Although he can be hot-tempered, Molten Man usually prefers helping Spidey to fighting him. But not always!

MS. MARVEL

⚡ RATING

FIGHTING SKILLS
●●●●●●○

SPEED
●●●●●●○

STRENGTH
●●●●●●○

High-schooler and Super Hero fan Kamala Khan developed super-powers after being surrounded by the Terrigen Mists. The mutation-causing vapor gave her stretchy super-powers and she named herself in honor of her favorite hero, Captain Marvel.

GOLD BRACELET HAS SPACE FOR KAMALA'S CELL PHONE INSIDE

FLEXIBLE SUIT, INVENTED BY HER FRIEND BRUNO

SPIDEY SECRET

Kamala believes that Super Heroes should help everyone who needs them—so she rescues her classmate Zoe from a river, even though Zoe is often unkind to her.

KEY ABILITIES

Name: Kamala Khan

- ☑ Stretching
- ☑ Shrinking
- ☑ Rapid healing
- ☑ Can alter appearance

FLEXIBLE HERO

Kamala's body can shrink, stretch, or expand to any shape. That's handy when teaming up with Spidey and the Champions.

46

MYSTERIO

Special effects expert and stunt man Quentin Beck wanted fame, so he turned to crime. He has no super-powers, so he uses tricks and illusions to fool people. But Mysterio is (generally) no match for Spidey.

⚡ RATING

FIGHTING SKILLS
●●●●●●●○

SPEED
●●●●●●●○

STRENGTH
●●●●●●●○

STAGE PROPS

Mysterio tries to pretend he has magical powers, but it is just clever stage tricks, props, and special effects. These illusions are mostly useless against genuine Super Heroes like Spidey.

HELMET PROTECTS MYSTERIO FROM SMOKE EFFECTS

SPIDEY SECRET

Mysterio is jealous of Spider-Man's fame and popularity. Once, he even tried to trick people into thinking he was Spidey!

MYSTERIO LOVES TO CONFUSE HIS FOES WITH SMOKE EFFECTS

KEY ABILITIES

Name: Quentin Beck

☑ Visual effects and stunts

☑ Basic hypnotism

☑ Acting

☑ Mechanical engineering

☑ Meticulous planning

NICK FURY

⚡ RATING

FIGHTING SKILLS
●●●●●●●○

SPEED
●●●●●●●○

STRENGTH
●●●●●●●○

A veteran of the US Army, Nick Fury is highly trained in combat and an expert in stealth missions. Now an agent of the secretive SHIELD organization, Nick is dedicated to doing what he believes is right.

NICK LOST AN EYE DURING HIS TIME IN THE US ARMY

SPIDEY SECRET

Nick Fury has recruited Spidey and many other heroes for SHIELD missions over the years.

KEY ABILITIES

Also known as:
Nick Fury Jr./Marcus Johnson
☑ Combat expert
☑ Durability
☑ Weapons expert
☑ Peak human strength

BLACK SUIT HAS A STEALTH MODE THAT MAKES HIM INVISIBLE

TOUGH BUT FAIR

When Nick first meets the young Peter Parker, he is a tough mentor. He wants Peter to become a truly great Super Hero.

NOVA

Sam Alexander doesn't believe his father's stories of his work in the Nova Corps, a team of space peacekeepers. However, when Sam puts on his dad's black helmet, he sees that it's all true. Now it's Sam's turn to be Nova.

⚡ RATING

FIGHTING SKILLS
●●●●●●○

SPEED
●●●●●●○

STRENGTH
●●●●●●○

TEEN TEAM

His newfound abilities makes teenage Sam a little arrogant. Ms. Marvel finds him very annoying at first.

ALL SAM'S POWERS COME FROM HIS NOVA HELMET

SAM CAN FLY FASTER THAN THE SPEED OF LIGHT

SPIDEY SECRET

ova forms the Champions Super Hero team with Miles Morales and Ms. arvel. They're determined to do good things.

KEY ABILITIES

Name: Sam Alexander
- ☑ Intergalactic flight
- ☑ Super-human speed
- ☑ Durability
- ☑ Control Nova Force energy

49

PENI PARKER

Peni Parker was raised by her Aunt May and Uncle Ben after her father died. Does that all sound a bit familiar? Well, in an alternate universe this brave middle school student is her city's spider-suited protector.

⚡ RATING

FIGHTING SKILLS
●●●●●●○

SPEED
●●●●●●○

STRENGTH
●●●●●●○

DOUBLE LIFE

When she's not battling Super Villains, Peni is just an average teenage vegetarian with too much homework!

SPIDEY SECRET

Peni's dad left her his SP//dr Suit. She uses her mind to pilot the suit, with a little help from a radioactive spider.

NO ONE SUSPECTS THAT THE SUIT IS PILOTED BY A KID!

ARMORED SUIT ALSO HAS A SNACK COMPARTMENT INSIDE!

🧠 KEY ABILITIES

Alias: SP//dr

☑ Strength
☑ Durability
☑ Web-shooting
☑ Resistant to damage (all while in armor)

PROWLER

Hobie Brown had lots great ideas, but no one noticed. Frustrated, the window cleaner turned to crime. He designed a costume and became his universe's Prowler. But, Spidey showed him that crime was not the best plan.

⚡ RATING

FIGHTING SKILLS
●●●●●●●○

SPEED
●●●●●○○○

STRENGTH
●●●●●●○○

NOT SO BAD

Hobie isn't cut out for crime, but his Prowler costume is well designed so he sometimes wears it to help Spidey out.

ARMORED SUIT PROTECTS PROWLER FROM INJURY

GAUNTLETS CAN SHOOT OUT A RANGE OF WEAPONS

KEY ABILITIES

Name: Hobie Brown
- ☑ Inventing gadgets
- ☑ Stealth
- ☑ Agility
- ☑ Computer hacking

SPIDEY SECRET

Hobie's plan to was to be a hero by stealing some money as Prowler and then returning it as Hobie Brown. Spidey spoiled that plan!

51

RHINO

Aleksei Sytsevich was just a regular villain until he took part in a secret experiment, which bonded a tough, rhino-like armor to his body. Now known as Rhino, he's fast, super strong, and virtually unstoppable.

⚡ RATING

FIGHTING SKILLS
●●●●●●●○

SPEED
●●●●●●●○

STRENGTH
●●●●●●○○

BRAINS VS. BRAWN

Rhino might be super strong but he's certainly not super smart or even very agile. Clever Spidey can usually defeat him.

IT IS HARD TO CAUSE RHINO ANY DAMAGE

RHINO CAN NEVER REMOVE HIS ARMOR, WHICH MAKES SLEEPING VERY UNCOMFORTABLE

KEY ABILITIES

Name: Aleksei Sytsevich

☑ Super-human stamina
☑ Resistant to injury
☑ Can go days without sleep
☑ Charging at foes

SPIDEY SECRET

Spidey has a simple strategy for dealing with Rhino—dodge him. The bulky villain cannot change direction easily.

RIO MORALES

Rio Morales believes in facing problems, rather than avoiding them. She tells her son Miles that their family does not run from things. However, she has no idea about all the Spidey-related stuff that Miles is dealing with!

RATING

FIGHTING SKILLS
●●●●●●○

SPEED
●●●●●●○

STRENGTH
●●●●●●○

BIG SECRET

Rio has no idea that the new Spider-Man is Miles. She thinks he is just worried about being at a new school!

KIND AND
LOVING
EXPRESSION

SPIDEY SECRET

Rio gets a big surprise herself when she discovers she's pregnant. Life with a baby and a teenager will be interesting!

NURSE'S
UNIFORM

KEY TRAITS

- ☑ Kind
- ☑ Hardworking
- ☑ Patient
- ☑ Brave
- ☑ Positive

53

ROCKET RACER

⚡ RATING

FIGHTING SKILLS
●●●●●●●○○○

SPEED
●●●●●●●○○○

STRENGTH
●●●●●●○○○○

Rocket Racer is a jet-powered Super Hero. He used to be a criminal, but Spidey helped him to realize that his talents would be better suited to helping people.

SPIDEY SECRET

Rocket Racer only turned to crime to make money to support his family. He has 6 younger brothers and sisters!

ROCKET CONTROLS THE SKATEBOARD VIA THIS HEADSET

KEY ABILITIES

Name: Robert Farrell
☑ Intelligence
☑ Inventing
☑ Resistant to damage (in suit)
☑ Rocket-powered punch (with gloves)

MAGNETIC BOOTS STICK ROCKET TO HIS JET-POWERED SKATEBOARD

THE RIGHT PATH

Rocket Racer and Spidey make a good team. And Spider-Man makes sure that Rocket is not tempted back into a life of crime.

SANDMAN

Sandman is former criminal William Baker. During a prison break he was accidentally exposed to radiation and his body became living sand. Sandman can shape-shift into any form or size.

⚡ RATING

FIGHTING SKILLS
●●●●●●○

SPEED
●●●●●●○○

STRENGTH
●●●●●●○

WORKING IT OUT

At first, Sandman used his powers to commit more crimes. Spidey eventually persuaded him to switch sides.

SANDMAN CAN BLAST SAND AT FOES

SPIDEY SECRET

During their first battle, Spidey got the upper hand by vacuuming up parts of Sandman's body.

KEY ABILITIES

Also known as:

William Baker, Flint Marko

☑ Shape-shifting
☑ Never needs to eat or drink
☑ Does not age
☑ Can become hard or soft sand

HIS MAIN WEAKNESS IS WATER, WHICH SOFTENS HIS SAND PARTICLES

HERO

SCARLET SPIDER

⚡ RATING

FIGHTING SKILLS
●●●●●●●○○○

SPEED
●●●●●●●○○○

STRENGTH
●●●●●●●○○○

Scarlet Spider is the most successful of Miles Warren's (aka the Jackal) spider clones. He was created to torment Spider-Man, but the two eventually became allies. Well, they do have a lot in common...

SMALL DIFFERENCE

Scarlet Spider has all the same abilities as Peter Parker, but he has added impact webbing and stingers to his arsenal.

SCARLET SPIDER HAS A SLIGHTLY DIFFERENT COSTUME

SCARLET SPIDER TAKES OVER FROM SPIDEY WHEN HE NEEDS TO

🧠 KEY ABILITIES

Name: Ben Reilly

☑ Spider-sense
☑ Super-strength
☑ Agility
☑ Healing

SPIDEY SECRET

Scarlet Spider took the name Ben Reilly to honor "his" aunt and uncle. Reilly is Aunt May's maiden name.

56

SCORPION

Scorpion is one of Spider-Man's oldest and most persistent enemies. He got his powers when he took part in an animal mutation experiment. It gave him the strength and agility of a human-sized scorpion.

RATING

FIGHTING SKILLS
●●●●●●○○

SPEED
●●●●●●○○

STRENGTH
●●●●●●○○

KEY ABILITIES

Name:
MacDonald "Mac" Gargan

☑ Super-strength
☑ Durability
☑ Agility
☑ Wall-crawling

SCORPION'S MECHANICAL TAIL HAS A STING AT THE END

SPIDEY SECRET

Before becoming Scorpion, Mac was a private investigator hired to find out more about Spidey.

HARD TO BEAT

His tough battlesuit with its deadly tail, plus his strength and speed, make Scorpion a dangerous foe. Just ask Miles Morales!

THIS BATTLESUIT PROTECTS SCORPION FROM DAMAGE

SHOCKER

⚡ RATING

FIGHTING SKILLS

●●●●●●●

SPEED

●●●●●●●

STRENGTH

●●●●●●●

Shocker is a thief and safecracker who used his time in prison to develop some useful gadgets. His "vibro-shock" gauntlets blast air that has been vibrated at a high frequency.

SPIDEY SECRET

Shocker uses his gauntlets to commit even bigger crimes than before, but Spidey is usually able to stop him.

🧠 KEY ABILITIES

Name: Herman Schultz

- ☑ Safecracker
- ☑ Engineer (self-taught)
- ☑ Vibro blasts
- ☑ Long-range punching (with gauntlets)

BELT CAN ALSO EMIT SHOCKS

PADDED SUIT PROTECTS SHOCKER FROM SHOCKING HIMSELF!

🕸 EXTRA SHOCKING

An outbreak of Spider-Virus caused Shocker to develop extra arms. It made it even easier for him to rob banks.

SILK

The spider that bit Peter Parker also bit another student, Cindy Moon. She discovered her powers when she accidentally webbed up her parents. A mysterious person then hid her away for many years to train her and keep her safe.

⚡ RATING

FIGHTING SKILLS
●●●●●○○○

SPEED
●●●●●○○○

STRENGTH
●●●●●○○○

WEB-SLINGERS

Cindy was kept hidden for more than 10 years. When she finally got out, she found Spider-Man and adopted the name Silk.

SPIDEY SECRET

Silk shares many abilities with Spider-Man but her "silk-sense" is even stronger than his spider-sense.

MASK HIDES CINDY'S TRUE IDENTITY

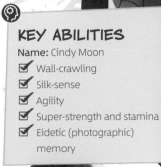

🧠 KEY ABILITIES

Name: Cindy Moon

☑ Wall-crawling

☑ Silk-sense

☑ Agility

☑ Super-strength and stamina

☑ Eidetic (photographic) memory

SILK'S WEBS ARE ORGANIC, MADE BY HER OWN BODY, UNLIKE SPIDEY'S

59

SILVER SABLE

⚡ RATING

FIGHTING SKILLS
●●●●●●○

SPEED
●●●●●●○

STRENGTH
●●●●●●○

As leader of the Wild Pack, Silver Sable's job is to hunt down international criminals and bring them to face justice. Although, unlike Spidey, she's a "hero for hire," Silver Sable believes she's on the right side.

HELPING OUT

Silver Sable and Spidey respect each other and have found themselves with a common foe on many occasions.

SILVER SABLE IS AN EXPERT WITH MOST WEAPONS

SPIDEY SECRET

Spidey is one of Silver Sable's favorite heroes to work with. He's strong and fast, and she trusts him completely.

COSTUMES ARE LINED WITH TOUGH, HEAT-RESISTANT KEVLAR

KEY ABILITIES

Name: Silvija Sablinova

☑ Martial arts
☑ Combat
☑ Acrobatics
☑ Strong leader

SKRULLS

The Skrulls are a race of alien warriors who love to build empires and take over galaxies. Their ability to shape-shift and assume any identity makes them very clever foes indeed. They'd love to take over Earth!

⚡ RATING

FIGHTING SKILLS
●●●●●●○

SPEED
●●●●●●○

STRENGTH
●●●●●●○

SKRULLS HAVE GREEN SKIN AND DISTINCTIVE POINTED EARS

SPIDEY SECRET

The Skrulls carefully planned a Secret Invasion of Earth by taking the identity of many Super Heroes.

KEY ABILITIES

Also known as:
Deviant Skrulls
☑ Shape-shifting
☑ Mimicry
☑ Flight
☑ Stretching and reshaping their bodies

SKRULL SPIDEY

The Skrulls' secret invasion made it very difficult to trust anyone. Even Spidey briefly fell victim to the cunning shape-shifters.

SKRULLS ARE RARELY SEEN IN THEIR TRUE FORM

SPIDER-GIRL

⚡ RATING

FIGHTING SKILLS
●●●●●●○

SPEED
●●●●●●○

STRENGTH
●●●●●●○

In an alternate future, Spider-Man's teenage daughter is a Super Hero. She faces a host of villains, including the Green Goblin's grandson, whilst also trying not to be late for school.

SPIDEY SECRET

In this timeline, Peter Parker has retired from his Spidey duties and May has no idea about her dad's past.

ARTIFICIAL WEB-SHOOTERS

KEY ABILITIES

Name: May "Mayday" Parker

☑ Enhanced spider-sense
☑ Wall-crawling
☑ Agility
☑ Basketball

MAY WEARS HER COSTUME UNDERNEATH HER REGULAR CLOTHES

FAMILY TREE

Mary Jane is May's mom. May inherited her red hair and outgoing personality, and her dad's spider-like super-powers.

SPIDER-HAM

In another universe, a spider was bitten by the pig May Porker after one of May's inventions went wrong. The bite turned the spider into a pig with spider abilities—aka Spider-Ham!

⚡ RATING

FIGHTING SKILLS
●●●●●●●○

SPEED
●●●●●●●●

STRENGTH
●●●●●●●○

SWINE-ING INTO ACTION

Spider-Ham defeats villains such as Ducktor Doom with some Super Hero friends—Captain Americat, Hulk-Bunny, Iron Mouse, and the Fantastic Fur.

MASK ADAPTED TO FIT PETER'S EARS AND SNOUT

🧠 KEY ABILITIES

Name: Peter Porker

☑ Spider-sense
☑ Agility
☑ Healing
☑ Durability

SPIDEY SECRET

Now known as Peter Porker, Spider-Ham lives with his adopted aunt May Porker. She's a scientist and inventor (not a very successful one).

SAME CLASSIC SPIDEY COSTUME, JUST IN A SMALLER SIZE

63

SPIDER-MAN 2099

⚡ RATING

FIGHTING SKILLS
●●●●●●○

SPEED
●●●●●●○

STRENGTH
●●●●●●○

In one possible future universe, a lab accident gives scientist Miguel O'Hara similar powers to Spider-Man. However, he also has fangs, sharp claws, and can move so fast that he seems to leave a copy of himself behind!

FAMILIAR FOE

Many of Spidey's old foes appear in Miguel's universe, too. He got the better of Scorpion by avoiding him!

WING-LIKE AIR FOILS ALLOW MIGUEL TO GLIDE SHORT DISTANCES

SUIT IS MADE OF A TOUGH MATERIAL THAT CAN WITHSTAND HIS CLAWS

SPIDEY SECRET

Miguel met Peter Parker, during a time-traveling adventure to 2211. They fought the Hobgoblin together.

KEY ABILITIES

Name: Miguel O'Hara
☑ Super-strength
☑ Agility
☑ Healing
☑ Telepathy

SPIDER-MAN NOIR

In an alternate universe, it's still the 1930s, a time known as the Great Depression. This Peter Parker lives his life in black and white. When a spider bite gives him super-powers, he is determined to help as many people as possible.

⚡ RATING

FIGHTING SKILLS
●●●●●●●○○○

SPEED
●●●●●●●○○○

STRENGTH
●●●●●●●○○○

THIS SPIDEY CANNOT SEE COLOR

KEY ABILITIES

Name: Peter Parker

☑ Wall-crawling
☑ Web-slinging
☑ Agility
☑ Stamina

HIS COSTUME LOOKS MORE LIKE A PILOT'S OR A DETECTIVE'S THAN A SUPER HERO'S

SPIDEY SECRET

Spider-Man Noir joins a team of Spider-people from alternate universes known as the Web Warriors.

NOT ALONE

There are many different Spider-people in alternate universes. Spider-Man Noir meets one with six arms!

65

SPIDER-WOMAN

⚡ RATING

FIGHTING SKILLS
●●●●●●○

SPEED
●●●●●●○

STRENGTH
●●●●●○○

Several heroes have taken on the name Spider-Woman, but Jessica Drew was the first. She got her powers when her scientist father gave her a special serum made from rare spiders to heal her when she was sick.

🧠 KEY ABILITIES

Name: Jessica Drew

☑ Wall-crawling
☑ Agility
☑ Healing
☑ Super-human hearing

SPIDER-WOMAN CANNOT FLY, BUT SHE CAN GLIDE

SPIDEY SECRET

Jessica can project powerful "venom blasts" from her hands to stun or permanently defeat her enemies.

JESSICA HAS HAD SEVERAL SUITS, BUT THIS IS HER SIGNATURE LOOK

BEING A HERO

Jessica has worked with Spidey in the Avengers. Once, she was secretly replaced by a Skrull for a while. The other Avengers noticed, eventually...

STARLING

Tiana Toomes is the granddaughter of the Super Villain Vulture. Although her grandfather designed her suit and taught her how to use it, Tiana follows her own path and is more likely to help Spidey than battle him.

⚡ RATING

FIGHTING SKILLS
●●●●●●●○

SPEED
●●●●●●●○

STRENGTH
●●●●●●●○

UNMASKING

Tiana meets Miles Morales when they're tracking the same villain. The teen heroes become friends and reveal their true identities.

VISOR PROTECTS TIANA'S EYES

ELECTROMAGNETIC WINGS ARE DESIGNED TO FLY WITHOUT MAKING ANY NOISE

KEY ABILITIES

Name: Tiana Toomes
- ☑ Flight (in harness)
- ☑ Super-strength (in harness)
- ☑ Tracking
- ☑ Artist

SPIDEY SECRET

Tiana also meets Peter Parker, who reveals some of the villainous things that her grandfather has done as Vulture.

SUPER TEAMS

Sometimes even Spidey can't defeat a foe all by himself—he needs a team of Super Heroes. He's joined up with some famous Super Hero teams over the years—and he's also faced some dangerous Super Villain teams, too.

AVENGERS

When Thor's brother, Loki, tried to trick Hulk, several heroes came to help. It was the start of the Avengers. The roster varies, but Spider-Man regularly helps out.

NEW AVENGERS

For a time, the original Avengers disbanded. So Captain America and Spider-Man formed the New Avengers with some other heroes. Unfortunately, one member, Spider-Woman, was secretly a Skrull at the time...

CHAMPIONS

When many Super Heroes took different sides in a conflict known as the Civil War, Miles Morales, Nova, and Ms. Marvel formed their own team—the Champions.

SPIDEY SECRET

Kang the Conqueror used a Spider-Man android to try and defeat the Avengers, but the real Spidey saved the day.

X-MEN

The X-Men are a team of mutant Super Heroes, formed by Professor Charles Xavier. Spidey joined the team for a while when his friend Wolverine was believed to be dead.

SPIDEY SECRET

Spider-Man is not technically a mutant, but he has a lot to offer the X-Men. He is asked to mentor the young mutants who are "most likely to become Super Villains"!

FANTASTIC FOUR

The Fantastic Four are Reed Richards (Mister Fantastic), his wife Sue Storm (Invisible Woman), Sue's brother Johnny (Human Torch), and their friend the Thing (Ben Grimm). They got their powers when they were exposed to cosmic radiation during a space mission.

SPIDEY SECRET

Spider-Man replaced his friend Johnny Storm in the Fantastic Four when the Human Torch was presumed dead.

B.O.E.M.

Founded by the Super Villain Magneto, the Brotherhood of Evil Mutants believes that mutants are superior to humans, and that mutants should take over the planet.

SINISTER SIX

The Sinister Six are a team of Super Villains who all share a common enemy—Spider-Man. The team was founded by Spidey's old foe Doc Ock.

TERESA PARKER

Teresa Parker is Peter Parker's long-lost, secret sister. Their parents kept her birth secret, and when they died, she was adopted. For years, Teresa has no idea about her true identity and Peter does not know that she exists.

⚡ RATING

FIGHTING SKILLS
●●●●●●○

SPEED
●●●●●●○

STRENGTH
●●●●●●○

BROTHER AND SISTER

Teresa first met Peter when she saved his life. The siblings are slowly getting to know each other.

WHEN NOT IN CIVILIAN CLOTHES, TERESA WEARS A SPECIAL SUIT

SPIDEY SECRET

Like her parents, Teresa is a trained spy. She has worked for the CIA and also SHIELD.

KEY ABILITIES

Name:
Teresa Elizabeth Parker

☑ Spycraft

☑ Flight (in costume)

☑ Driving and piloting

☑ Improvisation

AS A SPY, TERESA IS SKILLED AT BLENDING IN

70

THE THING

HERO

Ben Grimm was an astronaut and pilot until a space trip with his friend Reed Richards exposed him to cosmic radiation. He was transformed into a huge, rock-like hero. Known as The Thing, he is immensely strong.

⚡ RATING

FIGHTING SKILLS
●●●●●●●○

SPEED
●●●●○○○○○

STRENGTH
●●●●●●●○

SPIDEY SECRET
The Thing may look scary, but he is kind, gentle, and a good friend to many Super Heroes.

ROCK-LIKE SKIN CAN WITHSTAND MOST DAMAGE

THE THING IS SURPRISINGLY AGILE

🧠 KEY ABILITIES

Name: Benjamin Grimm

☑ Super-strength
☑ Durability
☑ Immortality
☑ Expert pilot

🕸 HELPING OUT

Spidey once needed the Thing's help to stop Hulk. They have also teamed up with the rest of the Fantastic Four.

THOR

⚡ RATING

FIGHTING SKILLS
●●●●●●●○○

SPEED
●●●●●●●○○

STRENGTH
●●●●●●●○○

Super Heroes don't come much mightier than Thor. Raised in Asgard, the home of the Norse gods, he's the God of Thunder. Thor was sent to Earth by his father Odin, and he helped to form the Avengers.

KEY ABILITIES

Name: Thor Odinson
- ☑ Durability
- ☑ Super-human senses
- ☑ Strength
- ☑ Nearly invulnerable

THOR'S MAGICAL HAMMER GIVES HIM EXTRA POWERS

THOR IS THE STRONGEST OF ALL THE ASGARDIAN GODS

SPIDEY SECRET

Thor is a brave and honorable hero. He respects Spidey and is happy to work with him in the Avengers.

MAGICAL HAMMER

Thor's hammer, Mjolnir, enables him to fly. He can also use it to control lightning. Thor is normally the only one who can use Mjolnir.

TINKERER

Phineas Mason is a brilliant engineer and inventor who hates Super Heroes. He thinks that they use their powers too recklessly. As the Super Villain Tinkerer, he uses his skills to make weapons and gadgets to stop them.

RATING

FIGHTING SKILLS
●●●●●●○

SPEED
●●●●●●○○

STRENGTH
●●●●●●○

ROBOT SUIT

Mason designed a special robot suit to trick Super Heroes and then attack them. Spider-Man was able to stop him.

TINKERER USES WHATEVER HE CAN FIND TO MAKE WEAPONS AND GADGETS

TINKERER TESTS ALL HIS INVENTIONS TO MAKE SURE THEY WORK

KEY ABILITIES

Name: Phineas Mason

- ☑ Scientific genius
- ☑ Inventing
- ☑ Smart businessman
- ☑ Making weapons out of regular household objects

SPIDEY SECRET

Tinkerer often teams up with other villains, such as Mysterio. He also sells his inventions to them.

TOAD

⚡ RATING

FIGHTING SKILLS
●●●●●●●○

SPEED
●●●●●●●○

STRENGTH
●●●●●●●○

Mortimer Toynbee is a mutant with an extraordinary leaping ability. As a child he was bullied for being different. Later, he joined the villain Magneto's Brotherhood of Evil Mutants and took on the name Toad.

FINDING FRIENDS

After his unhappy childhood, Toad is glad to make friends in the Brotherhood who are mutants, just like him.

KEY ABILITIES

Name: Mortimer Toynbee
- ☑ Super-human leaping
- ☑ Agility
- ☑ Flexibility
- ☑ Extendable tongue

SPIDEY SECRET

Spidey has met Toad a few times. He tries to show Toad that he can take a different path. So far, he has failed.

HIDDEN BEHIND HIS TEETH IS TOAD'S LONG, PREHENSILE TONGUE

TOAD HAS STRONG LEG MUSCLES TO ENABLE HIM TO LEAP

VENOM

Venom is an alien symbiote, a parasite that survives by attaching itself to another creature. Venom has had various hosts, but it keeps returning to Eddie Brock, a journalist with a grudge against Spider-Man.

⚡ RATING

FIGHTING SKILLS
●●●●●●○

SPEED
●●●●●●○

STRENGTH
●●●●●●○

VENOM'S FANGS AND CLAWS ARE ITS MAIN WEAPONS

KEY ABILITIES

Name: Eddie Brock
- ☑ Shape-shifting
- ☑ Absorbing powers from host
- ☑ Camouflage
- ☑ Stamina

VENOM CAN GENERATE WEBS

SPIDEY SECRET

The symbiote once bonded with Spidey. It acquired some of Spidey's powers before he realized what it was.

SPIDERS VS. VENOM

Venom might have spider-like powers, but he's no match for the combined might of Peter Parker, Miles Morales, and Ghost-Spider.

75

VULTURE

⚡ RATING

FIGHTING SKILLS
●●●●●●○○

SPEED
●●●●●●○○

STRENGTH
●●●●●●○○

Adrian Toomes was a late developer when it came to crime. After retiring from his job as an electrical engineer and inventor, he decided to use one of his creations to become a costumed criminal, Vulture.

SPIDEY SECRET

Spidey usually gets the better of Vulture, so Vulture often teams up with other villains to defeat him.

🧠 KEY ABILITIES

Name: Adrian Toomes
☑ Intelligence
☑ Invention
☑ Flight (in harness)
☑ Super-strength (in harness)

A WINGED ELECTROMAGNETI HARNESS ALLOWS VULTURE TO FLY

THE HARNESS ALSO INCREASES VULTURE'S STRENGTH

🕸 MATCH UP

Spidey has more super-powers than Vulture, but occasionally the older villain can outsmart him.

WOLVERINE

He has a reputation for being a grumpy loner, but Wolverine is also fearless and loyal. His super-strength, retractable claws, and ability to heal from nearly any injury have made him an asset to many Super Hero teams.

⚡ RATING

FIGHTING SKILLS
●●●●●●●○

SPEED
●●●●●●○○

STRENGTH
●●●●●●●○

SUPER TEAMMATES

Despite their different personalities, Wolverine and Spidey are friends. They work together in the New Avengers.

SPIDEY SECRET

Wolverine only trusts a few people, but his old pal Spidey is one of them.

WOLVERINE OFTEN WEARS A DISTINCTIVE BLUE-AND-YELLOW SUIT

RETRACTABLE CLAWS ARE MADE OF TOUGH ADAMANTIUM

KEY ABILITIES

Names:

James Howlett, Logan

☑ Mutant healing powers

☑ Super-strength

☑ Enhanced senses

☑ Super reflexes and agility

GLOSSARY

AGILITY
The ability to move quickly and precisely.

AKA
Also known as.

ALTERNATE UNIVERSE
A separate but in many ways similar world that exists in parallel (at the same time) as our own.

ANDROID
A robot that looks or acts like a human.

BULLY
Someone who is unkind or hurts those who are smaller, weaker, or different.

BURGLAR
Someone who breaks into a building to steal things.

CAMOUFLAGE
Something that helps you blend into your surroundings.

CLONE
An exact copy of a person or thing.

DURABILITY
The ability to last a long time without breaking or wearing out.

ENHANCE
Improve or make better.

GAUNTLET
An armored glove.

GENIUS
Someone who is exceptionally clever.

HYBRID
Something made by combining two different things.

ILLUSION
Something that is not what it seems to be; a trick.

IMMORTAL
Living forever.

INTEGRITY
Doing what's right.

INVULNERABLE
Impossible to wound or destroy.

MANIPULATE
To influence or control a situation to get what you wa~

MARTIAL ARTS
Styles of fighting used for sp~ or for self-defense.

MENTOR
Someone who gives trainin~ and advice.

MIMIC
To copy or imitate.

MUTANT
A person who is physically different from their parents because of a change in their DNA (information inside cells).

PREDATOR
An animal that kills and eats other animals.

PREHENSILE
Able to grasp or hold something by wrapping around it.

RADIOACTIVE
A kind of energy that can be very dangerous in large amounts.

REFLEXES
Actions your body makes without thinking.

REGENERATE
To regrow or replace a broken or damaged body part.

RELENTLESS
Without stopping or giving up.

RESOURCEFUL
Able to deal cleverly with new situations or problems.

ROOKIE
A beginner.

RUTHLESS
Cruel or without mercy.

SAFECRACKING
Breaking into a safe without the code or a key.

SHAPE-SHIFTER
Someone who can change the way they look to whatever they want, at any time.

S.H.I.E.L.D.
The Strategic Homeland Intervention, Enforcement, and Logistics Division, an organization that keeps the citizens of Earth safe.

SORCERY
Magic

STAMINA
The physical ability to do something for a long time.

STEALTHY
Moving or acting in a way that no one notices.

STRATEGY
A plan to achieve something you want.

SUPER-SOLDIER SERUM
A special formula that greatly increases a person's physical and mental abilities.

TACTIC
A way of achieving what you want.

TELEPORT
To travel across space or dimensions in an instant.

THWART
To defeat someone or ruin their plan.

TRACKING
To find someone or something, usually by following footprints or other traces of them.

Senior Editor David Fentiman
Senior Art Editor Nathan Martin
Production Editor Siu Yin Chan
Senior Production Controller Mary Slater
Managing Editor Emma Grange
Managing Art Editor Vicky Short
Publishing Director Mark Searle

Designed for DK by Lisa Sodeau

First American Edition, 2022
Published in the United States by DK Publishing
1745 Broadway, 20th Floor, New York, NY 10019

DK, a Division of Penguin Random House LLC
22 23 24 25 26 10 9 8 7 6 5 4 3 2
004–326312–May/2022

© 2022 MARVEL

A catalog record for this book is available from the Library of Congress.
ISBN 978-0-7440-4823-0

DK books are available at special discounts when purchased in bulk
for sales promotions, premiums, fund-raising, or educational use.
For details, contact: DK Publishing Special Markets,
1745 Broadway, 20th Floor, New York, NY 10019
SpecialSales@dk.com

Printed in China

For the curious

www.dk.com
www.marvel.com

MIX
Paper from
responsible sources
FSC™ C018179

This book is made from
Forest Stewardship Council™
certified paper—one small
step in DK's commitment
to a sustainable future.